FIRST TIME SEX TALES

EXPLICIT DIRTY EROTICA SHORT STORIES

STEFAN MCKINNIS

plicit Press

CHAPTER 1

FRENCH FUCKING FLASH PARTY

HECTORIA MILLETTE and Juliete Rique talked about their flash party they wanted to hold. They lay in bed in Juliete's bedroom, because Hectoria's Mom was very strict.

They lay on their bellies. Hectoria wore hot tight white short shorts and a pink blouse with black trim. She had not removed her white sneakers yet like Juliete. Hectoria's long frizzy blonde hair lay swept to the left side, over the front of her shoulder.

Juliete lay beside her in her short blue jean skirt and strappy little black and white blouse with tiny ruffles on the hem. Juliete's B cup breasts went into points. Those points formed tight nipples that rubbed against her bed sheet. She grew hornier as they talked.

. . .

Juliete whined, "Oh, Hectoria, where are we going to get the last three hundred dollars to pay the warehouse creep-- Iwan?"

"Where we always get the money, Juliete." Hectoria said, in her steady, sure voice.

"Mall Slutting." Brunette Juliete rolled over on her side and looked at Hectoria. "Why can't we get the money from somewhere else?"

"You want to work at McDonald's for a year."

"Ewwwww. Gross." Juliete shook her head. Her brown messy pigtails, high behind each of her ears, shook like rabbit ears.

"I've already got my half of the three-hundred." "Where! When!" Juliete pushed Hectoria playfully.

Hectoria pushed her hot girlfriend back off her side, onto her back. "You remember that older tutor who wanted to bang you?"

"Romem Campeaux, the college stud?"

"Yep. I told him, 'Pay me one-hundred and fifty dollars and you can fuck me'." "He did it just like that?"

"Juliete stop settling for fifty-dollar blow jobs. This isn't Fifty Shades of Gray." Hectoria got up and went back to Juliete's desk. She opened her laptop and started writing her college history paper again.

"I'm going to charge more. I must charge more."

"It's still light outside." Hectoria nudged Juliete, her oversexed girlfriend since fifth grade. They were not eighteen years old. They were in college. They were smart girls.

Juliete sat up and put on her black rollerblades. "I'll rollerblade around and if the guy looks clean and presentable and rich, I'll ask him." She turned to Hectoria staring into her laptop. "Call me when you get the money. I can book the warehouse from Iwan."

Juliete gave a thumbs up and went outside her house into the balmy summer air. The streets left plenty of places to rollerblade and search for Male-Money, as Juliete called it. Male-Money was money men willingly parted with if a hot chic gave them sex. Mall sluts got Male-Money all the time. Sure, it was a young girl thing, and she and Hectoria now entered the adult ranks--but fucking was fucking; sucking was still sucking. Fucking for Male-Money became the redline for her and Hectoria. They wanted to remain virgins until they entered college. Fucking was important. Sucking cock just felt good and gave the girls a huge ego boost.

As Juliete skated around, she looked at the men's crotches. She didn't want some boa constrictor cock jammed down her throat for one-hundred and fifty dollars. On the other hand, she certainly didn't know if she could take a huge eight or nine-inch prick up her pencil-thin overheating snatch either.

Several roller-blading guys approached her. They didn't have any money. She anticipated this and didn't waste much time on them. She stayed polite. Sometimes a cute boy's Dad or much older brother carried wads of cash in his pocket. She liked scouting. "I should become a model scout." This is how she introduced herself to several men without causing a riot. She spotted a man in a business suit by the train station. He read the paper. His spotless shoes and casually undone tie suggested he needed some relaxation. His cute dark curly hair fell every way on his head like a rocker. But he clearly carried a briefcase. He sat alone on the train bench. Juliete roller-bladed past him once, then twice. She stopped swirled and cocked her round brunette head to one side at the twenty-seven-year-old. "Ever consider becoming a model?"

"I'm probably too old to model. I'm twenty-three."

"Even better, I thought you were twenty-seven." Juliete always began by saying the men looked older than they looked. This kept their egos within her seventy-five dollar blowjob range. Also, they'd accept a one-hundred and fifty dollar price to fuck her. A stand-up fuck job in some alley, or cul-de-sac unnoticed by anyone. Perhaps even a deserted balcony is hidden away from the street. She pulled her pink cell phone out and snapped his picture. "I need this to send to my scout boss."

"I'm not interested," the guy said, his eye roamed up and down her body. "I am interested in you though."

Jackpot, Juliete said inside her mind. "Me? I'm not a hooker or Mall Slut."

Trickles of cum seeped out of her tingly narrow cunt into her white cotton panties as she thought about it. Was he the guy to take her virginity? Or did he just deserve a blowjob. "For seventy- five dollars, I'll give you a nice juicy blowjob."

. . .

The young businessman threw back his head and laughed. "You must be a virgin." "Why do you say that?"

"I can get a $50 or even $25 blowjob from a Mall Slut." "I'm a scouting agent."

"Have you ever slept with a male model?"

"I don't fuck them to get paid. The La Marineau Romantique Tableau Agence pays me."

He scoffed. He stared at the empty train tracks. He put his hands in his pocket, which Juliete took as a positive sign. He was trying to hold onto his cash.

Juliete smiled. "I'm a virgin. For five hundred dollars, you can fuck me?" "A virgin?"

"Five hundred dollars take it or leave it." Juliete's pussy grew wetter. Soon, she'd have a wet spot on her blue jeans. She stood up to walk away after a second. She lifted her left leg to skate off.

"Wait. You find a discreet place."

"Come with me." Juliete spotted a place not far. She took random pictures of Lancel Bourcier from various perspectives while skating backward, crossing his path, and from behind. "You're going to do well."

The place was off the street and across from a quiet park. "Stand there Lancel. Act natural. Look out into the park," Juliete said, while raising her blue jean skirt.

A brick wall surrounded them on two sides: back, and on the left. The front wall had a blue metal rail, but also a wall that went up to Juliete's waist. Her five feet, four-inch height made the place perfect. There was no way anyone could tell they were not a couple looking at the birds in the park.

Lancel opened his pants just enough to pull out his thick cock. "Lower my panties, Lancel."

He lowered her panties, squatting. He caught the whiff of her overheating pussy. When she stepped out of the panties, Lancel sniffed them and sighed deeply. "You smell good. Musky." Juliete blushed.

She had his money in her bra tucked under her conical breasts. She crossed her arms over her breasts and said, "Take my hymen!"

Lancel put her white cotton panties in his jacket pocket. He positioned his prick and pierced Juliete's sex. Lancel looked down and didn't see any blood, until he fucked her further up her cunt.

Juliete winced. "You've done it!"

Lancel looked down. He saw the blood on her gorgeous ass cheeks and the base of his cock. He pulled out more and realized he needed something to wipe up the blood. He retrieved Juliete's panties and proceeded to keep them both clean. Then he started rutting her tight channel again until he groaned holding onto Juliete's crossed arms, as they both stared into the park.

"That was worth it," Lancel said. "The most exciting thing I've done yet." "Me too, Lancel." She smiled.

"You know we don't have to end this . . ."

Juliete turned round. They disengaged. She snatched her bloody panties from Lance's hands. She wiped her inner thighs. "I'm open to a relationship, but the money I keep."

"The money is no problem, Juliete. I just want to stay with you--see where this goes." "Come to this party we're having tonight. Will you?"

Juliete told him where the party would be. She stood walking hand and hand in the park with Lancel. "Oh, I need to call someone, Lancel," Juliete called Hectoria. "Hectoria, I have the money!"

"I'm calling Iwan."

"Let the partying begin!" Juliete said.

CHAPTER 2

HAWAIIAN HONEYMOON

I AM one of the rare few that was actually still a virgin when they got married. My hubby and I had dated for a year before he asked me to marry him. I was thrilled beyond belief. I loved Randy from day one. I adored everything about him, in fact. He was handsome, charming, smart and sexy as hell! I had always had old-fashioned values, but I knew my body and myself. I knew that once my sexual tigress was unleashed there would be no stopping me.

Once Randy and I started dating seriously, I of course was turned on by him erotically and he was by me too. I keep myself in good shape; I have long red hair and green eyes. We fooled around quite a bit before we got married and I masturbated quite a bit, I will freely admit. In fact, my hubby and I used to mutually masturbate together while dating, or we would make homemade videos for each other and send them through email. This is how we made each other cum and stay sexually excited without me losing my virginity. You can imagine that by the time we got married, I was so ready for the honeymoon.

We had decided to spend our honeymoon on the beautiful island of Lanai in Hawaii. It was one of the more remote islands so my hubby and I booked 4 days and 3 nights in our very own private beach bungalow away from any others except some staff and a few restaurants and shops. After our wedding ceremony, Randy and I boarded an airplane to exotic Hawaii. I was so excited I was speechless, but more so because I was finally going to make love to and fuck the love of my life than the fact I was going to visit one of the most romantic and beautiful places on earth.

After a long flight, we finally made it to our romantic hideaway and it was all that the brochures and travel agent had promised and more. It was decorated beautifully in ocean blue and turquoise hues against crisp white walls and pastel blue carpeting. It was like a beach inside the bungalow.

We could open French doors and windows revealing the lovely salt air and the sound of the waves crashing upon the shore.

I will never forget the first night I ever made love with the man of my dreams. It was magical and so hot, I will never forget one detail of it. I showered and put on my sexy black lace lingerie trimmed in pink eyelet lace. I put my red hair up in a loose French knot. I put minimal makeup on - a dusting of glimmering pink eye shadow, a touch of mascara, and carnation pink lipstick. I put my black stilettos on as well just to make me feel like a sexy woman about to get fucked hard by her new hubby.

When I walked into the bedroom area, my hubby had lit vanilla-scented candles all over the room giving it a romantic glow. The lace curtains blew with the ocean breeze giving the atmosphere a balmy yet cool ambiance.

Randy was lying on the silk cream-colored bed spread with the canopy billowing gently in the wind as well. He wasn't wearing one shred of clothing and he looked so sexy. Here lied the man I loved and craved.

"You look, beautiful baby," He said with his hazel eyes growing wide in anticipation. I noticed his sexy cock was becoming a boner very quickly as well. He stroked it tenderly as I walked up to him and revealed my big tits to him with my pink nipples pointing straight out like his cock. I slipped my stilettos off and joined my new husband in our marriage bed. Randy slid his greedy fingers underneath my black lace panties and began fingering me gently, then harder. He used 1, 2, 3, and then 4 fingers as I rode his palm like crazy. I rubbed my love button vigorously on his hand while he finger fucked me. I pulled and teased his cock head and rim, and we kissed deeply and our tongues mimicked our bodies motion.

I was getting wetter by the second and his dick was so hard I thought it might break into two pieces. I could tell it ached to be inside my wet snatch. I craved to be fucked every way Randy could fuck me. He slipped inside me slowly inch by wet inch and made me moan like a puppy. He put my long legs up by his ears and looked down as he went in and out slowly grazing my g-spot on the way in and the way out. He'd hesitate and make me beg for more g-spot stimulation. I could feel my cunt drenching his prick head as he pulled out inch by excruciating inch.

I never imagined making love could feel this amazing and hot. I knew Randy was the most incredibly erotic man on earth but the way he felt inside of me blew my mind. I could feel my cunt lips gripping his boner as he seductively swiveled his hips in and out of me. I wanted to be fucked on my knees too so I flipped over and let him enter my pussy from behind. "Baby your cunt looks so fucking hot grabbing my dick like a mouth," he said as he began to fuck me harder.

I turned my head to see him pumping me and his eyes revealed his height of erection and arousal. I have seen him before his hot cock shoots off and he gets an unmistakable look within his hazel eyes, and he was gaining that look now. I felt him plunge deeper and my lips grab tighter. His balls began to slap my ass as he increased his fucking velocity. He sucked on my sensitive neck making me squeal like a schoolgirl. His hands were on my tits, pulling my nipples until I thought I was going to cum by that alone. I knew he and I were about to have an orgasm in unison.

When he started twisting them my cunt convulsed, and my pussy shot a small splash of cunt juice on his stiff shaft, which only made him hornier. He knew when I came I was going to soak the bed and him but I didn't care, his cock was taking me to places no woman had ever been before. It was as if I could see it penetrating me from the inside.

Suddenly l felt him stiffen and a growling groan escaped his lips as he pumped stream after stream of thick cum inside my cunt. My pussy exploded from the drenching he was giving my greedy hole. I heard the gush splash against his stomach and cock and watched it run down off him onto the sheets.

After hours of making love and fucking, we finally collapsed in a post-orgasmic duo onto the bed. My cunt still twitched as my cum and his bubbled out of my cum cave. I was not disappointed in sex at all and I loved Randy more now than ever before. I had a feeling he and I were going to have years of sexual pleasure ahead of us and I for one couldn't wait.

CHAPTER 3

INNOCENCE LOST

THE LAST OF the patrons moved out of the parking lot. It was just after eleven-thirty and the late-night liquor joint would close in half an hour. Inside it was an awkward young man she knew from school. They had sat near one another in biology but they weren't friends. Nathan was too tall for his age, and strange and reserved. He wore glasses and looked every bit like the son of a Polish immigrant father and an American mother. Helen needed nothing more from this odd boy except that he gets his high school graduate cock hard and sticks it inside her until she was no longer a virgin. He would also need to have the stamina to go one more round post-breaking so that he could give her a solid reference for non-virgin sexual intercourse.

Helen was herself a geek. But she was a cute geek so she was accepted by most of the circles at school. She had just been so focused on getting the grades that got her into an Ivy League school that she hadn't had time to lose her virginity. But now that she was going to a college that would have its share of intelligent jocks wanting an uncomplicated first year, she was not about to risk being the boring weird girl holding on to her virginity. Her pussy wasn't sacred to her. She knew that she wanted to have her share of decent sex at college herself and so she needed to free herself of this limitation. So Helen took her tight ass and virginity all wrapped up in a short summer dress that sat way above her knees and walked into the store when she was sure nobody was there.

Nathan gives her a casual wave as she enters and then walks around looking for nothing. She walks around the store for ten minutes before he finds her in the beer aisle and offers her some help. There is a tension between them that she knows comes mostly from her. She wants to just ask him to fuck her but the thought of him saying no and then telling everyone is something that would be worse for her than if she arrived at college on Sunday a virgin. She had always known that everyone got reckless on Friday nights, but she was never one of them. Helen had never been "everyone" and now she was at a loss as to how she would seduce this *total loser* as she'd heard him called. They stare at each other for another ten minutes, Nathan confused by the looks he's getting, and Helen afraid that Nathan would at any minute tell her to leave and close the store. This was her only chance with this dude. She knew from his mother, friends with her mother, that Nathan was leaving for his college the next day.

"Can I help you, Helen?" Nathan was getting worried.

She could think of nothing else now and so she turned and walked towards the cash desk. Nathan followed. He then went behind the counter to serve her, once she decided what she wanted. She took a pack of condoms and gave it to Nathan. He gave a look, smiling with his eyes. She tried to look sure of herself as he rung up the purchase.

"Who's the lucky guy?" Nathan could think of nothing

else to make her feel less awkward. She gives him a stare before answering, "You are!"

Nathan takes less than five seconds to process his luck and walks around the counter to the condoms. He gives her another look, another smile, and then takes a pack marked *extra-large*. He then gives this pack to her before closing up the store a minute early. He turns the lights off and Helen follows him to the office in the back that had a TV and a bed for when the staff needed to rest between shifts.

He takes his clothes off, everything including his boxers, revealing immediately why he needed the supersized condoms. His cock was nowhere near erect but looked to be at least twelve inches thick. Helen is nervous now but undresses to her panties and bra, an innocent white. She sits on the bed and folds and unfolds her arms a few times. Instantly Nathan understands what it is that brought him this treat. He knows that all she wants is his cock, and that she would rather fumble with a fool like him so that by the time she got to the big boys she was a whole lot less awkward. He knows that she is about to use him. He can't help feeling sorry for her. Firstly, he isn't a virgin. And secondly, since she clearly is, his cock might be very uncomfortable for her.

Virgins are always a treat, so Nathan decides to be that awkward first experience for Helen. He doesn't give away that he's on to her jig though, jumping straight into the deflowering. He gets on his knees in front of her and runs his hands over her thighs. He kisses her knees and then her thighs, before biting into the side of her belly. She squirms, panting because the feelings are new and fantastic. She gets the immediate sense that she might have underestimated

Nate and that he might have done this before. After brief embarrassment, she is relieved that he will know what to do with her, especially given the size of his cock. She resolves to do whatever he asks. She's just going to follow his lead.

He blows warm air over her the part of her panties that covers her cunt. Immediately she starts to jerk involuntarily, shocked by the sensation and surprised even more by her reaction to this sensation. She feels like her pussy has suddenly been filled with warm custard and a ticking timer. Nathan gently pushes her onto her back and rids her of her panties. Her pussy is now open and exposed to whatever Nathan has in mind for her next. He moves his hands over her thighs and then between them, parting her legs so that the sense of exposure is almost overwhelming.

She closes them instinctively, Nathan gently urging them apart again. She concentrates on keeping them open now, since that is what is needed.

The first lick sends such a wave through her that she screams. Nathan smiles to himself as he turns up the music in the office before returning to her cunt and giving it a few more licks. He decides not to talk to her, just to be aware of any sign that she is uncomfortable or wants to stop. He gives her virgin pussy a few more licks until she becomes familiar with the sensation. When her screaming becomes moaning he knows that he can move to the next step. He gives her cunt an appreciative look and then wets the tip of his index in his mouth. He runs the finger in small circles on Helen's perfect clit until it comes to full bloom. Her moaning now is as loud as her screaming was. After another dip into his mouth, Nathan eases the tip of the finger into her pussy. She lets out a loud gasp, sitting up straight, her eyes on her cunt and the finger moving into it.

Nathan forces a little more of his finger into her while

getting up so that he sits next to her and immediately goes for her lips. He holds her head to his, his hand in her hair massaging the back of her head as he does the one thing she is familiar with. Helen kisses him back, expertly. She'd always been such a great kisser that nobody dared guess she was a virgin. She's always made out so well with guys at parties. The familiarity of kissing relaxes her quickly, and Nathan takes advantage of this, pushing the rest of his thick index into her cunt. Slowly, while still kissing her, he fucks her with this finger, moving it all in and almost all out of her vagina in the hopes of heating and wetting it all at once. He achieves this.

Very slowly, he lets her have two fingers in her. His index and middle work themselves into her slow and gentle. They kiss deeply while Nathan gently stretches her cunt, pushing against her virginity without breaking it, simply stretching her pussy as far back as possible. She starts to recognize the sensation, having touched herself enough to know that soon she will be cumming, her body shaking and heated. She holds on to Nathan tightly as she anticipates that he will bring her to this state with his fingers. He fingers her for a while longer and then removes his fingers from inside her with great care. She shakes, but not for an orgasm, but for the realization that she won't be having one, yet.

Nathan pulls on his cock so that it is rock solid and then runs a condom down over it. He has nothing but his own spit to wet his cock with and so this is what he uses. Again, there is panic on Helen's face. But Nathan tells her not to worry and lays next to her so that they are both on their sides but facing each other. He starts to kiss her and then tells her to concentrate on nothing but his lips now. He lifts her top leg and places his cock between her thighs before letting the leg drop again. Nathan kisses her deeply while fucking her thighs, getting her familiar with his rhythm. She enjoys the feeling of the thick cock in between her legs, brushing against her cunt. Suddenly she wants the solid tool inside her, although she has no clue what this will really feel like. Nathan keeps thrusting, kissing; occasionally putting his fingers on her cunt again, and then in it. His dick starts to throb for all the promises of pussy.

Nathan's hand is on his cock again, guiding it, brushing then intensely ribbing the thick head against her clit and then the entrance to her. He starts to push his cock into the hole, kissing her harder now, with heated distracting passion. He gives one swift thrust forward and his cock is inside her, just the head and a few inches. Then both his hands are on her head, holding their heads together, and his tongue deep in her mouth. He thrusts gently, slowly turning her onto her back and mounting her. She tenses at the thought that his full weight on her will drop his entire cock into her. But he just keeps thrusting gently, adding no more cock than is already inside her. He just moves his lips to her breasts now and turns them into fiery sensuous mounds of pleasure.

He moves his one hand down to her thighs, propping himself up with the other hand so that she isn't force-fed cock by accident. He parts her legs and takes her one leg in hand, throwing it over himself. Unsure, she throws the other leg over him as well. He gives her a smile, and then as he kisses her again, slowly drives his shaft into her until it is at her wall. He pulls back, still kissing, and goes for the wall again. He gives her dozens of these preparatory thrusts until he can no longer hold his own cock back and sucking hard on her tongue Nathan drives his dick straight through her wall. Her legs wrapped tight around him as her body contracts. Nathan pauses for a minute and then thrusts into her newly deflowered cunt until every cell in her body relaxes and she takes his twelve hard inches into her with ease. By the time they leave the shop, they've used all three condoms in the pack.

CHAPTER 4

LILIJA AND THE RUSSIAN OLIGARCH

LILIJA CHISTYAKOV LAY on Russian Oligarch, Vasilid Pavlov's huge king-size bed. The Russian Oligarch feasted his eyes on Lilija's pert eighteen-year-old tits. Her tits defied gravity. And defying things was something Lilija loved to do; buck the rules, bend the rules, and reshape the rules. She went to an exclusive Russian Girls High School. Her crumbled blue and white checked skirt lay on the floor. Her white bra was on top of her skirt. She wore a 34-B bra and her development wasn't over yet. Her soft, doughy breasts continued to grow. Vasilid noticed this as he watched her pinch her puffy nipples. Quarter-size coral areolas supported her hard eraser-sized nips. Lilija loved to masturbate. She would have gone home and masturbated even if Vasilid's proposition wasn't as attractive as it was.

"I'll give your Dad enough money to start his own oil business," the short white-haired Vasilid had said in the rich studio size bathroom. He slipped into the bathroom when he saw Lilija go in. She sat on the toilet tinkling, her blue and white mini-checked panties hugging her ankles. Her schoolgirl skirts up around her waist.

. . .

Lilija always liked Vasilid's style of dress. Dark gray business slacks, jackets, white dress shirts, and black alligator shoes. He wore the most delightful cologne "St. Petersburg for Men." He smelled like the Russian woods in wintertime.

"My Dad has enough money from his jewelry business," Lilija responded, undisturbed by Vasilid's presence. He stood with his back to the bathroom door, leering at her long blond hair tied in two ponytails, one behind each pretty pink ear. She shook her head no. She rolled off the toilet paper and wiped herself. She started to pull up her panties.

"I'll pay you one hundred dollars for your dirty panties." He counter-offered.

"You really want to fuck me." Lilija said, pulling her warm panties around her 32-inch hips. She possessed a flat tight tush. She lowered her skirt over her panties stopping Vasilid's lingerie show.

"Yes, fucking you'd be splendid." He moved closer to her.

Lilija knew he hated scandals. She didn't fear him attacking her. "I have a bad reputation at school for saying what I think." She turned to the mirror, leaving Vasilid to step closer up behind her as she retouched her lip gloss. Lilija fixed her eyes in the mirror on Vasilid as he came closer.

"What shall I tell your Dad, Lilija? Yes or No?" He hugged her gently. He nuzzled his chin to her neck. He raised her ponytails off her shoulders and kissed each one. "Humm?"

. . .

"I'll marry you, Vasilid, if you help my Dad." She put her lipstick away inside her black shoulder-strapped purse.

"Marriage is way too formal." He kissed the back of her head and turned her around to face him.

Lilija smelled the mint on his breath. He always smelled good. "We are at an impasse. But I'll sell you my panties for one-hundred dollars—that should satisfy you for now."

"I'm a businessman. I travel. I work." He picked up her hands and kissed them. "I don't have time for relationships."

Lilija pushed him away. "Then why have you come to me?"

"I thought a wild, fast girl like you would understand. Passion. Fucking for the moment. The thrill of the chase."

"I'm not a common whore. I fuck because the guy might love me." She reached for the doorknob.

Vasilid grabbed her wrists. He reached into his pocket and took out the money.

Lilija stopped, reached under her school skirt, and squatted low lowering her panties. Once her panties were around her black Mary Jane's, she lifted her feet removing them. She held her warm panties on her index finger. She held them high right under his nose. "I masturbated in them earlier in the day." She smirked. "I should charge more."

Vasilid took the panties as Lilija took the money.

. . .

He sniffed her panties. "I've dreamed of this moment, soon as you graduated from high school." "I, too, dreamed of fucking you." She said, putting the money inside her purse. "I'd be the perfect wife for you Vasilid. A hard-nosed bitch with a mind for making money."

"I own a lot of things. None of them dominate me."

Lilija reached out and hugged Vasilid. She stood three inches taller than her five feet six inches. Her blue eyes smoldered with passion. The same passion she saw in Vasilid's eyes.

"Decide."

"Yes. I'll marry you, but first I must have you tonight. Now Lilija!" He pressed her hard against the door. The golden doorknob rattled. Lilija watched as Vasilid's eyes jumped nervously. "Relax, Vasilid." She held up her black purse. "My purse hit the door handle."

Vasilid smiled. He rubbed his hands through his stark white hair. He moved in and kissed Lilija on the lips. She spread her legs wide. Her scent flowed. She kissed him back. She broke away and said, "Fuck me now Vasilid. Before I change my mind!"

Vasilid raised her skirt. He turned her suddenly around facing the wooden door, with its long spoon-shaped doorknob. Lilija giggled. He unbuckled his pants. He licked his fingers and parted her flat ass cheeks. Lilija knew a little bending motion easily exposed her swollen pussy lips. She pushed her ass out and arched her back. Vasilid's prick found her pussy groove. He rapidly slid his dick meat up and down her surprisingly wet slit.

"You're wet as a whore." "No, wet as a virgin."

"I'll see about that." He forced himself up to her love sheath only to find after a couple of pushes he was unable to go further. "By the saints, you're a virgin!"

"You paid a good price." She pushed back in a jerk and broke her own hymen on Vasilid's fifty-year-old prick. Her blood flowed over his hard cock.

Vasilid found going slow impossible. He started fucking her faster as if she was a common whore.

"That's better. Use me!"

Vasilid's small hands grabbed her waist harder and brought her to his hips. He held her there grinding against her young eighteen-year-old body. His other hand mauled her young tit.

"I love your tits."

"They're all yours Vasilid," she gasped. "Just make me cum. Do me! Harder!"

Vasilid fucked like he was eighteen again. His desire feasted on the smell of her ponytails hitting him in the face. Her legs flexing back on his red-stained cock. He smelled the iron of her blood. Her tight love space yielded slower and slower. He finally reached her cervix and blasted his volcanic hot goop up her hot snatch.

"I'm coming!" Lilija said. "Touch my tits!"

He kept fucking as one hand twisted her nipples.

Lilija reached down, pressed her clit, and stroked five short times and she turned. She laid her shoulders on the door and turned on the hot water. She screamed out as Vasilid came, too!

One year later, Lilija's Dad bought an oil manufacturing business, and Lilija and Vasilid were married. Lilija taught Vasilid that relationships eased life; they did not make life harder. They are happy and plan to have a child in one year.

CHAPTER 5

VIRGIN FOREST

MY NAME IS MEGAN. I'm still a virgin at age 18. It is because my strict parents had thought they could prevent me from knowing carnal pleasure forever. They forgot that I could travel around the world without leaving my room. I could just imagine their faces growing livid with rage if they came to know I'm no longer a virgin. I was "devirginized" via cybersex. In fact, I can call myself an expert. My online boyfriend Jim taught me all I need to know, especially how to play with myself to reach my orgasm.

He usually watches me while I danced and slowly undressed before the webcam. Then I masturbated as Jim also fondled himself. We agreed to tell each other what pleasured us most, so we could pretend that we were making love to each other for real. I am a master of pleasuring myself through Jim's guidance.

Jim had more exciting things in mind after a month, though. He urged me to use a vibrator, which he had managed to smuggle to me through the post. I had to collect the item myself from the post office.

It was a huge silicon dildo that had a clit stimulator. I

was so excited to use it, so I emailed him quickly to *"please come online"* that night.

When he did he had already an enormous erection. I swallowed with eagerness as I was sure I would feel that delicious dick inside my aching pussy this time.

I put on the slow music and undulated my hips sensuously, swaying to the beat. I caressed my breasts and fondled my pussy through my negligee. My nipples stood proudly through my blouse, bursting to free themselves from their confinement. I let go of my last shred of clothing and sat on my bed to spread my legs.

Jim was staring at me fixedly through the webcam, his cock standing upright and angry. He was caressing his shaft up and down with his fingers.

We had our earphones on and I whispered:

"Honey, please eat me."

Jim wasted no time. He hissed, breathless, into his device, "Babe, I'm spreading your legs wide. You're on the edge of the bed, and I'm kneeling, my tongue on your labia."

"Oh hon, yeah, yeah, run your tongue up and down my pussy. It feels so good."

As I was saying this, I was touching my pussy, running my fingers up and down my labia, and up my clitoris, rubbing feverishly. I had closed my eyes and imagined Jim giving me those pleasurable sensations.

· · ·

"I'm inserting my fingers into your slick pussy, while sucking and licking your clit," he said hoarsely.

"Yeah, that feels so good, babe," I moaned, indicating my delight, as I inserted my fingers into my already moist vagina. I imagined him sucking my clit, and I pulled the protrusion with my fingers, simulating a sucking action.

"I want you to sit on my lap, so I could fuck you and fondle your tits and clit too," he said lustily. "Now wet the dildo with your lips; imagine it is my penis," he continued.

I felt my pussy quiver with excitement as I sucked and ran my tongue along the shaft of the dildo. He gasped seeing me lick the crown of the dildo and sucked it again.

"Ahhhh," he groaned. "Come and ride me, babe," he said wildly. "I'm starting to sit on your lap," I murmured incoherently.

I was hyperventilating with extreme eagerness.

I started inserting the dildo, "I'm going down on you now," I was breathless with lust.

My vaginal opening was still tight, so when I inserted the dildo I did it slowly. I could feel my pussy warmly enveloping the dildo as I pushed it in and out. The sensations caused by the friction of the dildo with my tight vaginal walls, the pressure on my G-spot, and my clitoris, were beyond words.

My pussy became somewhat sore, but when I pushed the dildo in and out of my tight love tunnel, my juices made it easier, and the friction created responses in my body I had never imagined. I was moaning and thrashing wantonly, spreading my legs further apart to accommodate the huge, delicious dildo.

Jim was increasing the tempo of his fingers on his shaft. His face was red with passion, and I knew he was so aroused.

"I'm thrusting in and out of your tight and wet pussy," he prodded me. "Oh, you're so tight babe, hmmmm."

"I'm thrusting faster and harder now," his voice made me hotter, and I let out a loud gasp as I increased the speed of the in and out movement of the dildo inside my pussy.

"Harder hon, harder and faster," I urged Jim, as I pushed the dildo deeper into my pussy, then pulled it all the way out, and then pushed it all the way in again."

"I'm fucking you harder and faster," Jim responded. "Ahhh, you're so tight, so sweet, so hot, hmmmm."

He had also increased his tempo with his hands.

I started to tremble when my orgasm peaked, "I'm coming… oh god," I gasped. "Harder please, harder," I cried as I plunged the dildo deep into my vagina with quick, strong strokes.

"I'm cumminng too," he groaned.

Then I felt my world explode with incredible delightful sensations that blinded me. I was stuttering and gasping, and my body continued jerking as I savored the dildo still moving in and out of my pussy.

I had to press the clit stimulator for several minutes and wiggled the dildo round and round my pussy, to savor the waves and waves of superb pleasure coursing through my whole body.

Jim was groaning loudly too, while he massaged his penis and his semen spurted into the air, victorious and free. He collapsed in the chair, his penis still in his hand, as his throes of an orgasm slowly subsided.

"I love you, baby," he finally whispered, when his breathing returned to normal.

"I love you too, hon," I huskily uttered, basking in the afterglow of our cyberspace lovemaking. I was officially devirginized, and it was an unforgettable, delicious experience.

ABOUT THE AUTHOR

Stefan McKinnis is an emerging erotica author of many erotica kinks and sub-genres. Be sure to check out other books and leave a review if this story got you hot!

Visit my blog at Stefan McKinnis Blog

Join my newsletter for exclusive Stefan McKinnis Newsletter

Sign up for Free Stories from Xplicit Press Authors

Xplicit Press Author Updates

Like Xplicit Press on Facebook

Follow Xplicit Press on Twitter

Readers: I want to expand a few of the stories to see where the characters can be explored further. If there are any of the stories that you would like to read more about again, I'd love to hear from you!

Keep In Touch
Stefan McKinnis
info@stefanmckinnis.com